My Grandma Could do ANYTHING in Hawaii!

by Ric Dilz

Mahalo to all the Grandmas
in the world.

Rein designs inc.
Boulder, Colorado

Art & Design by Rein Designs Staff

My Grandma
could do
ANYTHING...

My Grandma
doesn't bungee jump
from a helicopter...

But she could!

My Grandma
doesn't jump as high
as a dolphin...

But she could!

My Grandma
doesn't ride a bike
down a volcano...

But she could!

My Grandma
doesn't lead a
hula show...

But she could!

My Grandma
doesn't surf a
20 foot wave...

But she could!

My Grandma
doesn't
juggle pineapples...

But she could!

My Grandma
doesn't windsurf
with whales...

But she could!

My Grandma
doesn't swim as fast
as a humu...

But she could!

My Grandma
doesn't build a
giant sandcastle...

But she could!

My Grandma
doesn't play a
ukulele...

But she could!

My Grandma
doesn't dive as deep
as a turtle...

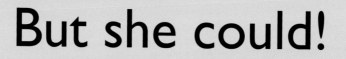

But she could!

My Grandma
doesn't bring a rainbow
home for me...

But she could!

My Grandma
could do lots of things,
but I'm so happy with
the one thing she does
the best...

Can you find these Hawaii friends in this book?

humuhumunukunukuapua'a

sergeant major

yellow tang

teardrop butterfly fish

dolphin

sea turtle

monk seal

gecko

moorish idol

humpback whale

nēnē

octopus

Can you find the pictures that go with these Hawaiian words?

ahi–fire
`āina–land, earth
ānuenue–rainbow

hala kahiki–pineapple
hōkū–star
honu–turtle

kahakai–beach
koholā–humpback whale

keiki–child or children; kids.

lei–garland of flowers, leaves,
    nuts or shells
limu–seaweed

mahina–moon
makai–ocean, ocean water
mele–song
mauka–mountain

moku–island
moana–ocean, sea

nai'a–dolphin
nalu–wave
niu–coconut

pālama–palm tree
pali–cliff
pulelehua–butterfly

tūtū–Grandma
ukulele–stringed instrument,
    small guitar

wa`a–canoe
wai–water (not salt water)

Visit www.reindesigns.com
for more fun products!

Published by Rein Designs, Inc.
Boulder, Colorado

ISBN 0975870424

Library of Congress Control Nunber: 2006904071

Printed in China